For [redacted] School —

Enjoy the adventures of
Gertrude!

—Ginger Doyel
11/7/02

Gertrude

The Albino Frog

And Her Friend *Rupert* The Turtle

Written by Marcia A. Silvermetz
Illustrated by Ginger Doyel

ISBN 0-9718724-0-6
LCCN 2002107435

Copyeditor: Jen Behe
Illustrator: Ginger Doyel
Graphic designer: Alexandra Littlehales
Project consultant: Jeri Goldstein, The New Music Times, Inc.
Education specialists: Drs. Anne Perkins and Kate Keeling of Christopher Newport College

Disclaimer: People with this condition prefer to be called "people with albinism" rather than albino. No intention of insult has been implied or inferred. Please contact the National Organization of Albinism Hypopigmentation if you are interested in more information. There actually are albino frogs. They are pinkish-white and their eyes appear red in certain types of light. Contact your local pet shop for more information.

Attention all corporations, gift shops, libraries and professional organizations: volume quantities are available at limited discounts. Profits from hardcover and softcover books are donated to worldwide children's charities. For financial information, please contact Kathleen Rice of PhaseAccounting@yahoo.com

Printed and bound in USA.

HICCUP COTTAGE PUBLICATIONS
subsidiary of Wavecrest Enterprises, Inc.
Post Office Box 311
Charlottesville, Virginia 22902 USA
hiccupcottage@yahoo.com
www.hiccupcottage.com
(434) 980-5347

Acknowledgements

My grateful thanks go to the following people who believed in this project from the very start: To my spiritual friend Ginger Doyel, without you this project would have stayed a dream. To my advisor Deborah Strzepek, without you there would be no dream. To my clients at Wavecrest Fitness and Massage for teaching me about receiving by allowing me to give.

Many thanks to Erin Johnson for coaching me through hard times; to Kathleen Rice for enriching my life with universal love; to Jeri Goldstein for helping me deal with the little things; to Kathy Kildea, a true biscotti goddess, for real nourishment; to Vikki Bravo with utmost royal respect and thankfulness to her mitzvot; to Michele Kupfer for climbing mountains and her husband Gary and family for support; to Margie Swanson for lighting and guiding my way; to Mary Rieber for running hills of life with me; to Linda and Wayne Thomas for pure love and entertainment; to Alie and Mase Sanford for graceful conversation; to Dusty Armstead for continuous belief; to Betty Simon for long, short and curly tales; to Vanessa Ochs for helping guide my spiritual journey; to Sarah Chisdes for friendship and support; to Sherry Kraft for understanding, listening and fun runs; to Lake Monticello potluck group for fantastic conversations; to Angela Mulloy for heartfelt expressions of kindness; to Hiawatha Green for serving, protecting and caring for me; to Nancy Shotwell for years of perspective; to Ken Nail for website help; to Candace Krevansky for belief and support; to Elsa Paulsen for unconditional love; to Nelson Teague for legal giggles; to Doug Cox for adjustments and dear friendship; to Monika Piland for stress reduction; to Tony at Chaps for giggles, coffee and ice cream; to the Colonnade's seniors for great fun and fitness; to all of CBI for spiritual comfort; to Paul Novelli for lifelong love and friendship.

In Michael Hampton's memory for joyous and unique difference; to Magic and Lucy, and in memory of Schuyler, for unconditional love. And finally to all of you for helping to perfect the world through the purchase of this book.

Dedicated to my parents Rita and David who understand
tolerance, to my brothers Mark and Barry who help me
practice it, to Tanta's little ones, Jacob, Hallie and Avi who
are learning to live it, to my sister-in-law Carole who teaches
it, and to the curious, unusual, and unique living beings in
this universe for their courage to be seen and looked at and
for their right to be listened to and heard.

It is a tree of life for those who grasp it,
and all who uphold it are blessed.
(Siddur Sim Shalom)

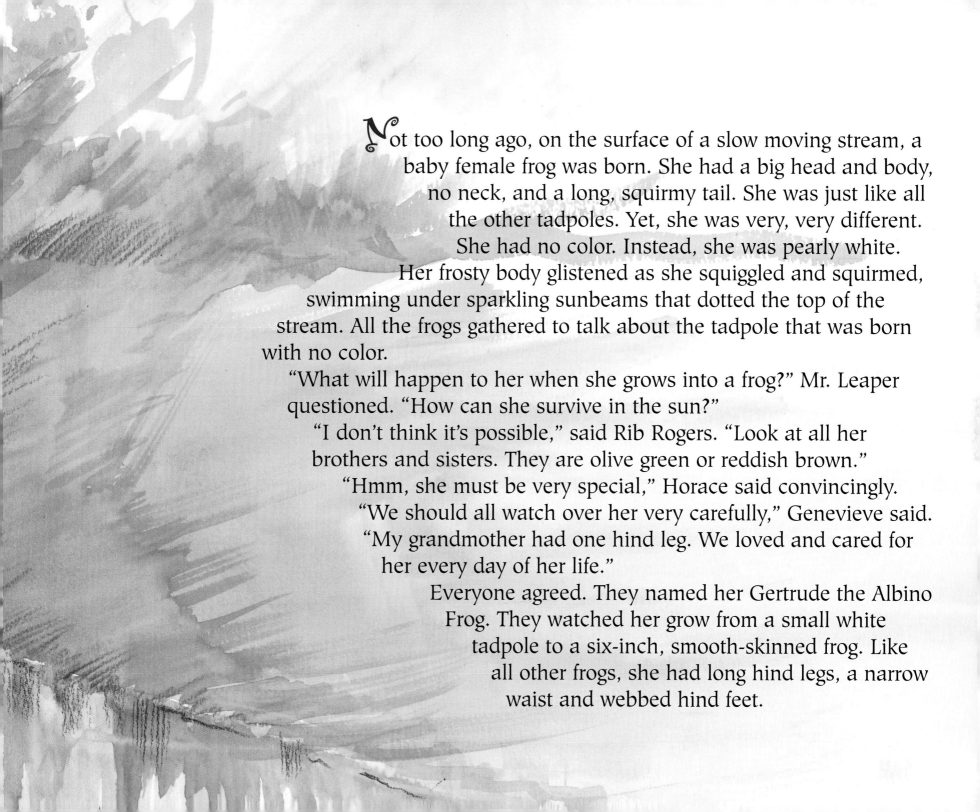

ot too long ago, on the surface of a slow moving stream, a baby female frog was born. She had a big head and body, no neck, and a long, squirmy tail. She was just like all the other tadpoles. Yet, she was very, very different. She had no color. Instead, she was pearly white. Her frosty body glistened as she squiggled and squirmed, swimming under sparkling sunbeams that dotted the top of the stream. All the frogs gathered to talk about the tadpole that was born with no color.

"What will happen to her when she grows into a frog?" Mr. Leaper questioned. "How can she survive in the sun?"

"I don't think it's possible," said Rib Rogers. "Look at all her brothers and sisters. They are olive green or reddish brown."

"Hmm, she must be very special," Horace said convincingly.

"We should all watch over her very carefully," Genevieve said. "My grandmother had one hind leg. We loved and cared for her every day of her life."

Everyone agreed. They named her Gertrude the Albino Frog. They watched her grow from a small white tadpole to a six-inch, smooth-skinned frog. Like all other frogs, she had long hind legs, a narrow waist and webbed hind feet.

Gertrude did almost everything any other frog
could do. But she needed to stay in the shade. An upside
down lily pad perched on a vine was her shady home.
She wore a wide straw hat, so big it covered her head,
eyes and ears and dipped down to shade her back. She
tucked orange feathers into the right side of her hat.
They were a gift from the Robin Bird Family.
She also wore large green sunglasses, given to her by
the spectacle shop, to protect her delicate eyes.
She carried a parasol made of soft, light green lily
pads. It gave her extra protection from the sun.

Everyone loved Gertrude, but
she still felt lonely. Her school friends
were able to run, jump and play all over the
lily pads. They climbed on to dry land, bounding
out of sight. How her legs ached to stretch over land
and bask in the hot sun!
She wished the sun didn't burn her delicate skin.
She yearned to jump as high as heaven, plopping and
splashing her webbed toes through spring rain
puddles. But instead, she watched
the other frogs play.

"I wish I had a special forever friend to play with this summer," Gertrude thought. "We could play under the hanging leaves and shaded lily pads. We could scramble from one rock to the next, near my moist and shady home. Then we could drink tea and eat cookies together."

"Oh, well," she sighed.

Soon summer arrived and the frogs were ready for their annual Town Fair, which was filled with fun and games. Gertrude always found the shadiest spot during the fair. She sat under a large Weeping Willow tree close to the pond so she could watch the fun.

First was the croaking contest. Only young male frogs competed since they could make the deep "jug-o-rum" sound. The female frogs judged the contest.

"Jug-o-rum," groaned one young male, barely making a sound.

"Listen to Cary croak!" said one judge.

"He'll win some year," said another.

The tongue-flicking contest was next. Many frogs entered. That was always fun.

"All right," Phillip the umpire said. "When I blow my whistle, it means start flicking. Who can catch the fly the fastest this year?"

Lily won last year, but Henrietta outflicked her this time.

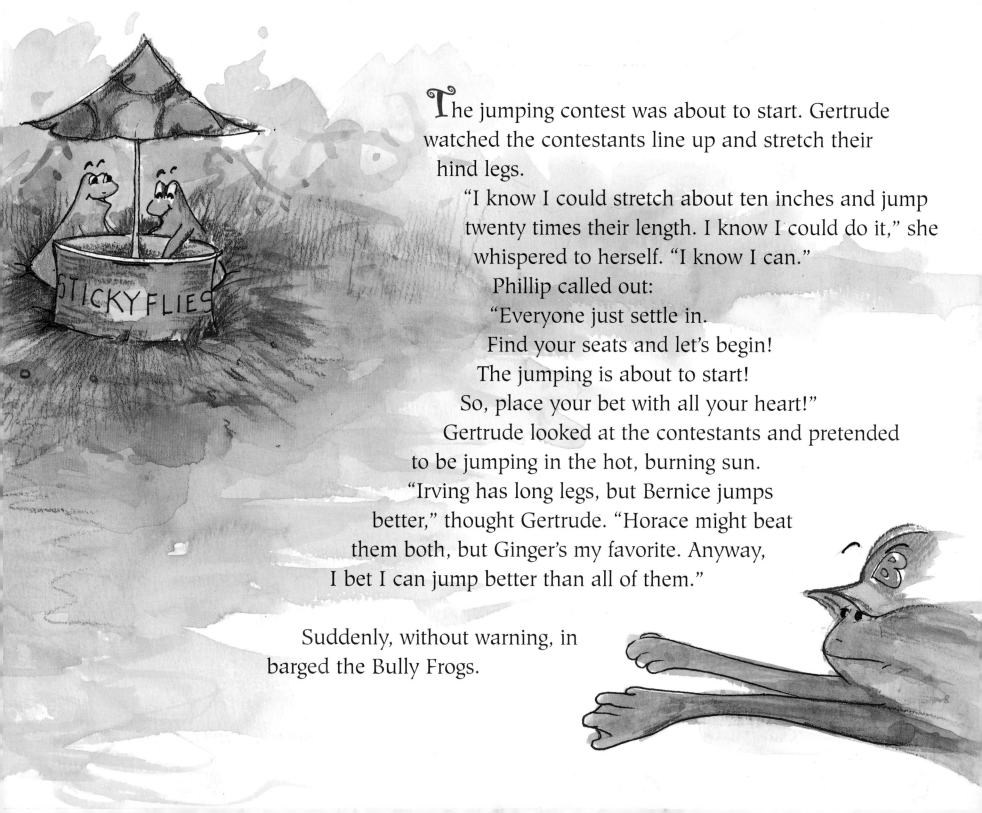

The jumping contest was about to start. Gertrude watched the contestants line up and stretch their hind legs.

"I know I could stretch about ten inches and jump twenty times their length. I know I could do it," she whispered to herself. "I know I can."

Phillip called out:

"Everyone just settle in.
Find your seats and let's begin!
The jumping is about to start!
So, place your bet with all your heart!"

Gertrude looked at the contestants and pretended to be jumping in the hot, burning sun.

"Irving has long legs, but Bernice jumps better," thought Gertrude. "Horace might beat them both, but Ginger's my favorite. Anyway, I bet I can jump better than all of them."

Suddenly, without warning, in barged the Bully Frogs.

ive Bully Frogs hopped through the crowd. They bulldozed down the ice cream stand. They spit melon pits at everyone. They cackled at the older frogs. Then they stood over Gertrude, pointing and laughing.

"You look so silly dressed in your wide hat and green sunglasses," said a Bully Frog.

"Jug-o-rum, you little white frog," said another. "You don't fit in here. No one here is white. Everyone has a color. Look at the green and red and brown on everyone. You don't fit in!"

"You can't even jump in the contest," said another Bully Frog. "Ha, Ha, Ha!"

Laughing out loud, they jumped away.

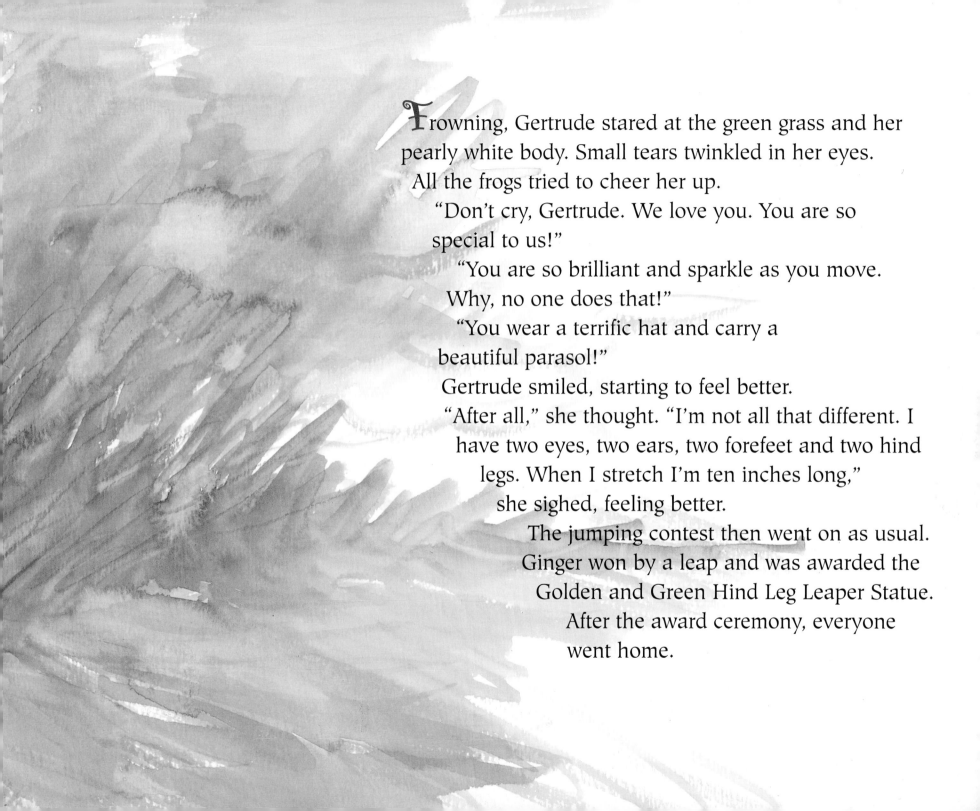

Frowning, Gertrude stared at the green grass and her pearly white body. Small tears twinkled in her eyes. All the frogs tried to cheer her up.

"Don't cry, Gertrude. We love you. You are so special to us!"

"You are so brilliant and sparkle as you move. Why, no one does that!"

"You wear a terrific hat and carry a beautiful parasol!"

Gertrude smiled, starting to feel better.

"After all," she thought. "I'm not all that different. I have two eyes, two ears, two forefeet and two hind legs. When I stretch I'm ten inches long," she sighed, feeling better.

The jumping contest then went on as usual. Ginger won by a leap and was awarded the Golden and Green Hind Leg Leaper Statue. After the award ceremony, everyone went home.

One cloudy day, while strutting down Pond Place, Gertrude needed to rest. She spotted a small hill. It was well shaded by a large oak tree. She jumped right on top of it and sat down.

Suddenly, the hill moved!

"Who is sitting on my back?" A voice spoke from under the hill.

"Oh, my!" Gertrude was startled. "This hill talks! I'm Gertrude."

A turtle stuck his head out. Gertrude was sitting on his shell. He turned his head and smiled.

"Hi, Gertrude! Don't be scared of me! I am Rupert the Turtle. Excuse me, but why aren't you jumping and bounding out in the fields like all the other frogs?"

"It's so nice to meet you, Rupert. I hope you don't mind my sitting here so comfortably. It seemed so cozy. You see, I am an albino frog. I cannot go in the sun or I will burn. When I leave my shady lily pad home, I always wear my wide straw hat and green sunglasses."

"Gertrude, I am so pleased to meet you. We are almost alike. I'm the only turtle in this part of frog country. Although I can go outside, I am most comfortable and peaceful in my shell. I like to be covered by my shady hard top!"

Gertrude and Rupert became very good friends. She had found her special forever friend.

Rupert was very understanding when Gertrude told him how it felt to be different from the others. He would cry whenever Gertrude told him sad stories and laugh whenever something funny would happen. He got angry when Gertrude told him about the five Bully Frogs.

Sometimes the Bully Frogs would come straight up to Rupert when he was giving Gertrude a ride home. They would be mean to him, too.

"Ruby, Ruby, Rupert baby in a shell!"

"Hiding in your little shell, Rupert?"

"Rupert is the friend of an albino frog!"

"Turtle, turtle in a shell, Rupert, Rupert you do smell!"

"Eewwww!"

Then, they would jump away.

One day, after the Bully Frogs bothered them, they headed back to Gertrude's home.

Rupert had an idea that would make both of them feel better.

"Gertrude, why couldn't we have this summer's Town Fair closer to your home? Maybe the jumping trials could be under the shade of the Weeping Willow tree. We could time the frogs jumping from lily pad to lily pad. Then, you could be in the contest!"

Gertrude was so excited by the idea that she jumped up and down, almost slipping off Rupert's back.

"You could be my coach and wear a whistle and a stopwatch!"

"Yea!" said Rupert. He loved the idea of being her coach.

They soon forgot about the rude Bully Frogs.

Everyone loved the new contest idea. The pond near Gertrude's home became busy with frogs practicing. Gertrude was very happy and served plenty of tea and cookies.

Every day the Bully Frogs hid behind the Weeping Willow tree. They watched while Gertrude jumped and Rupert timed her.

"What do you think this new jumping thing is about?" asked a Bully Frog.

"I don't know," answered another. "But look at that white frog go! I had no idea she was that good! She doesn't seem any different from any of us."

"It looks like this year's jumping contest is different from the usual ones," said another Bully Frog. "It looks like fun."

"Do you think they would let us play, too?" wondered another.

The Town Fair was the following Sunday afternoon. Everyone was bubbling with excitement.
Phillip started speaking:
"Come one, come all, the Fair's about to begin! Come see, come hear. Everyone can win!
Today is filled with games and fun. Come one, come all, come everyone!"
The croaking contest was first.
"Jug-o-rum." All the young boys tried to make the deep, croaking sound.
The tongue-flicking contest was next. There were so many new contestants that there was a tie.
Finally, came the new Lily Pad Hop. Gertrude was the first to line up.
"Wow! Look at Gertrude stretch!" The frogs were so impressed. They were excited and happy to
see her compete. They cheered loudly. Rupert was very proud of her. He felt important with his
stopwatch and whistle hanging around his neck. He looked happily around the crowd, and then
back at the contestants. Then he saw three of the Bully Frogs lining up for the contest, too.
He got very nervous.

"Oh, no!" Mr. Leaper exclaimed. "Look who is going to compete with all the other frogs!"

Mr. Leaper was leery. He wondered if this was a plan to ruin the new Lily Pad Hop.

He saw two Bully Frogs standing behind the crowd.

Phillip spoke to everyone:

"Time to hop from pad to pad.

Line up with me girls and lads.

Any more contestants ready to hop?

Come line up here ready to bop.

It looks like many will try to win.

Let's start the contest, shall we begin?"

Before he blew the whistle to start the race, he waited a moment to see if any others would join. The two Bully Frogs left in the crowd looked at each other.

Phillip hopped into the crowd and whispered to them:

"Go now and join the rest.

Show them you can do your best.

Gertrude is trying to fit in. Go on, you, too, can try to win!"

With that, the two nodded to each other and jumped up to join the group.

The whistle squealed.

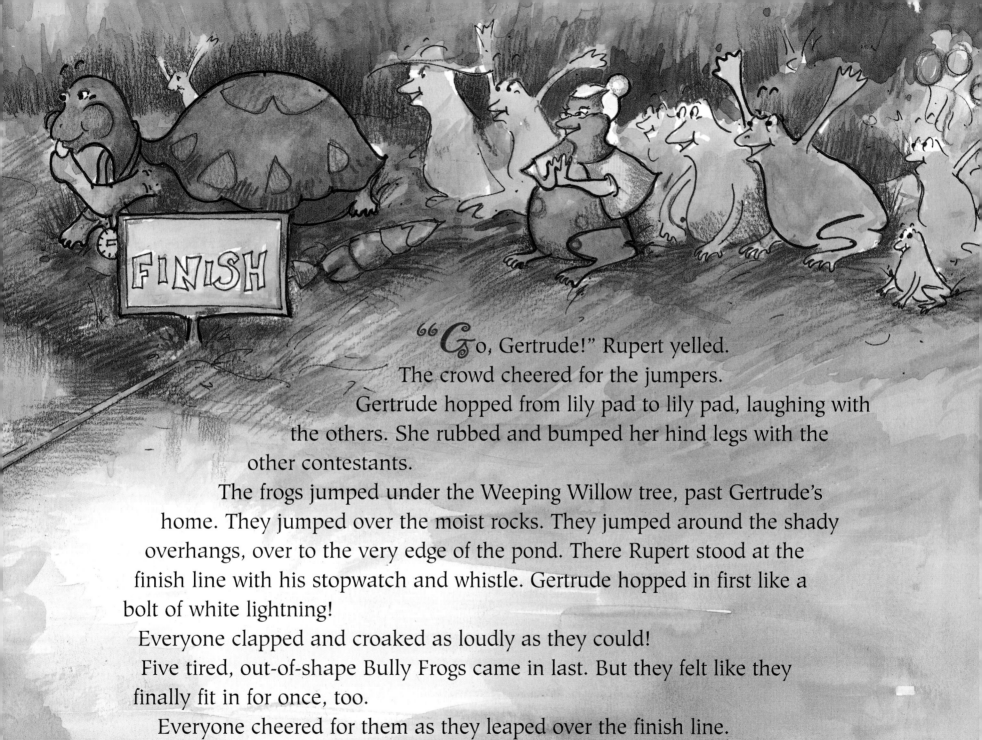

"Go, Gertrude!" Rupert yelled.

The crowd cheered for the jumpers.

Gertrude hopped from lily pad to lily pad, laughing with the others. She rubbed and bumped her hind legs with the other contestants.

The frogs jumped under the Weeping Willow tree, past Gertrude's home. They jumped over the moist rocks. They jumped around the shady overhangs, over to the very edge of the pond. There Rupert stood at the finish line with his stopwatch and whistle. Gertrude hopped in first like a bolt of white lightning!

Everyone clapped and croaked as loudly as they could!

Five tired, out-of-shape Bully Frogs came in last. But they felt like they finally fit in for once, too.

Everyone cheered for them as they leaped over the finish line.

Phillip smiled and spoke to the
crowd again:
   "You see how easy it can be
to fit right in with such glee?
No one needs to laugh at others;
we are all sisters and brothers.
Gertrude wins the hopping prize,
though with Rupert she surely ties.
Without him to think of change,
this contest might not have been arranged:
a chance to join together as such,
and love our community just as much.
Thank you Bully Frogs for joining in;
difference is definitely where we win.
You can be yellow, green or white;
you can be loud and full of might.
But when we compete on equal ground,
we are all equal: this we found!
Thank you for coming to the Fair.
Next year will bring a brand new dare!"

Gertrude proudly
rode home on Rupert's back.
She carried the Golden and Green Hind Leg
Leaper Statue with glory. The five Bully Frogs
hopped happily behind. They slapped each other on their backs. They offered
compliments and congratulations to each other, to Gertrude and to her coach Rupert.
Sitting in Gertrude's home, they all enjoyed the evening's brilliant yellow, red, pink and orange
sunset. Laughing and talking together, they drank tea and ate cookies. They were happy being
with each other.
They were all different, yet they had become very special forever friends.

About the Author

Marcia A. Silvermetz completed her Master of Education degree in Sports Medicine/Exercise Physiology in 1981, at the University of Virginia, Charlottesville, Virginia. She completed her Bachelor of Arts degree in Psychology/Biology in 1979 at the University of Albany, Albany, New York.

In her years involved in Sports Medicine, her work centered around pain management, cardiac rehabilitation, massage and fitness programs for injured and rehabilitating clients. She has been professionally published over thirty-five times in national, international and local journals, magazines and newspapers, including: *The Clinical Journal of Pain* (Mayo Clinic), *The International Journal of Athletic Training, The Virginia Journal, Accent on Living, Cooking Light* and on CD ROM with *Social Issues Resource Series, Inc., Natural Jewish Parenting* and *Hopscotch The Magazine for Girls.*

In addition Marcia has owned a fitness studio and has had a local television fitness show. She worked with The Pain Management Center, at The University of Virginia, where she created, directed, promoted and managed the Physical Education and Aerobic Research Center. She helped create the Central Virginia Fitness Center in Orange, Virginia and helped develop a Cardiac Rehab unit in one of the top 100 hospitals in the country, Culpeper Regional Hospital, Culpeper, Virginia. She currently teaches balance and fitness to residents of The Colonnades, a senior living community in Charlottesville, Virginia, and is the exercise physiologist at the Federal Executive Institute of Charlottesville, Virginia. In addition, Marcia also owns Wavecrest Fitness and Massage.

She has also applied her pain management medical massage skills to the treatment of horses and riders through her business called Stable Relationships.

Marcia continues to write for children and older adults, and she raises dogs. She lives in Charlottesville, Virginia.

About the Artist

Though born in Richmond, Virginia, Ginger Doyel began painting at the age of three while living in Scotland. Her career as a professional artist began in 1997 when she illustrated *Annapolis: the Guidebook* by author Katie Moose. Since then she has illustrated several children's books including *Queen Sniffertiti and the Nuzzlepup Orchestra* by Lane Nelson and *How Charlottesville Got Its Theater Back* for Charlottesville's historic Paramount Theater.

Returning from her travels to Annapolis, Maryland, Ginger studied Landscape Architecture at the University of Maryland and explored golf course design. After transferring to the University of Richmond's reputable Jepson School of Leadership Studies, graduating first in her class, she was awarded the James MacGregor Burns award for excellence in Leadership Studies.

Ginger's greatest joy of being an artist is the way it enables her to connect and invest in youth. She has facilitated six Youth Lead sessions as part of a grant given by the Verizon Foundation. Through this program, Richmond's inner city youth created murals of the city of Richmond, Virginia.

Ginger presently operates a full time golf art business called Art Fore Golfers and has worked as an artist with the Professional Golf Association Tour.

Ginger lives in Annapolis, Maryland.

ORDER INFORMATION (or visit www.hiccupcottage.com)

$19.95 per book
Shipping and handling: $4.50 per book, add $2.00 for each additional book.
Add Virginia state taxes (4.5% of subtotal).

Please photocopy and return by mail to Hiccup Cottage Publications to order *Gertrude The Albino Frog And Her Friend Rupert The Turtle*

NAME _____ QUANTITY _____

ADDRESS _____ COST PER BOOK _____

TELEPHONE _____ SUBTOTAL _____

SHIPPING _____

TAX _____

TOTAL _____

Checks or money orders made out to Hiccup Cottage Publications.

Please mail to:
Hiccup Cottage Publications
Wavecrest Enterprises, Inc.
Post Office Box 311
Charlottesville, Virginia 22902
hiccupcottage@yahoo.com
(434) 980-5347

For nonprofit orders, please contact Hiccup Cottage Publications for special discounts.

Thank you for your order. Profits from hardback and softbacks books are being donated to worldwide children's charities. For financial information, please see copyright page.

Thank you for helping to repair and perfect the world.